My Mom's Not Cool

Written by

Rubi Nicholas

Illustrated by

Maia Chavez Larkin

Blueline Publishing LLC

Denver, Colorado

My Mom's Not Cool

Written by

Rubi Wahhab Nicholas

www.rubinicholas.com

Illustrated by

Maia Chavez Larkin

http://verlichtstudio.blogspot.com

Designed by

Pamela McCarville

www.allusallthetime.com

©2008 Blueline Publishing LLC

Denver, Colorado, U.S.A.

www.bluelinepub.com

Text© 2008 Rubina Wahhab Nicholas

Illustrations© 2008 Maia Chavez Larkin

Printed in China

ISBN 978-0-9776906-4-0

Rubi Nicholas

As a first-generation American Muslim woman of Pakistani descent, Rubi Nicholas is the antithesis of what one would expect with such a strong ethnic background. Born into a culture steeped in the tradition of the quiet, compliant female, Rubi breaks the mold. Far from choosing the typical life as an obedient wife, she has walked a variety of career paths, has chosen a non-traditional family route and now has succeeded in breaking even more rules as a stand-up comedian.

Selected in 2006 as Nick@Nite's "Funniest Mom in America," Rubi demonstrated that her unique point of view and warm, friendly style can bring together all kinds of people through her charming charisma and clear sense of timing.

Rubi's humor incorporates her ethnic heritage, her family life as a corporate woman whose husband is a stay-at-home dad, and the antics of their two little girls. Her ability simultaneously to weave her story, to allow the audience into her life, and to reveal the ways in which we can all find common ground is a remarkable talent. From politics to parenting, culture clashes to kids, Rubi understands what makes us laugh.

Originally from Pennsylvania, Rubi lives with her husband and two little girls in Castle Rock, Colorado. She has an MBA in management information systems and two MS degrees from Temple University, and a BA from Villanova.

Maia Chavez Larkin

Maia Chavez Larkin is an illustrator and journalist. Daughter of oil painter Eva Van Rijn and the late WPA muralist and National Academy of Design member Edward Arcenio Chavez, Maia hails from a creative and peripatetic family. Born and raised among artists, she was initially trained in architectural illustration at the New York School of Interior Design and went on to study painting and drawing at Il Chiostro near Siena, Italy.

Her classical pen and ink work has shown at the Kiesendahl + Calhoun Contemporary Art Gallery in Beacon, New York; the Fletcher Gallery in Woodstock, New York; and the Broome Street Gallery in Manhattan, among others. As a commercial illustrator, she has worked for the Beaver Creek Resort Company, the Seven Lakes Lodge and the Adoption Exchange, as well as for various periodicals. She and her husband, a fellow journalist, live in Denver, Colorado, and are in the process of adopting their first child.

Acknowledgements

This book is dedicated to the coolest people I know:

Sophie and Yasmin - my cool girls

Ted - the coolest husband ever

Samina - for her own personal cool

Uzma - the coolest little sister in the world

Pam, Giselle, Kari, Kim and Gina - the cool moms of Sand Wedge

Heather - the coolest fake mom a kid could have

Wahhab - cool dads raise cool daughters,
who become cool moms - thanks dad

Zarina - who taught me how to be a mom
in the first place ... you are so cool

Foreword

This book is for kids and moms, and for everyone who's ever thought their mom wasn't cool. I guess that means it's really for all of us. While every mom out there is doing the very best that she can, sometimes it seems that another mom has found a different path. It's not right or wrong, just different. I tell my girls every day, "everyone has their own style," just to remind them that there is no right way to live. Each of us has our own story, our own triumphs and tragedies, and the more we learn to appreciate all that we do have – life's little joys – the better off we are. That's what this book is about, to remind ourselves that the choices moms make are irrelevant when it comes to loving our children.

Moms do all they can to show their children love. In this story, it's singing a lullaby. In your story it may be an evening prayer, Saturday morning pizza for breakfast, or taking a huge bubble bath together. It may be a game of catch, or a tea party with stuffed animals – whatever style you choose, acts of love are counted each day by our children. Though they might get into mischief, test our boundaries or push us to the brink of insanity, they always have a stronghold on our hearts. Guess what? The favor is returned. No matter how uncool your kid thinks you are, deep down that kid knows how it feels to be loved, and sees the things you do to show that love. Children and moms alike, celebrate your love, your special bond and your own style!

Part of the proceeds from this book will be donated to women's charities that are focused on the health and well-being of mothers.

Rubi Nicholas

Every day when I wake up,
my mom makes me eat breakfast.
I'm not allowed to eat macaroni
and cheese for breakfast.

My friend Samantha can eat whatever she wants for breakfast, and she doesn't even have to sit down. Her mom is so cool.

My mom's not cool.

When my mom drops me off at school, she kisses me, right in front of everyone.

My friend Olivia's mom gives her a high five.

One time, I was at her house, and her mom let her eat her dessert before dinner! Her mom is so cool.

My mom's not cool. Half the time we don't even have dessert at our house.

In the summer, I still have a bed time!

My mom says, "bed time in the summer is the same as all year long."

Amelia's mom lets her stay awake until after dark in the summer. Amelia's mom is so cool.

It's not fair!
When I am in bed,
I can hear Amelia
playing outside.

Every night before I go to bed, I have to brush my teeth and wear my pajamas.

My friend Sophie gets to sleep in whatever she wants.

Sometimes, she sleeps with just a t-shirt on. Her mom wears a t-shirt too.

She is so cool. My mom's not cool — she wears a robe that says "countin' sheep" on it.

When my mom lies down next to me, she reads me a story. Then she rubs my back and sings "You Are My Sunshine" over and over again.

When she does that, I don't care about anything. I don't mind that my friends get to do things that I don't. I feel really happy and warm and gooey in my belly.

So — my mom's not cool, but I still love her more than any other mom in the world.